For Dearest Angela

With all my Love for a
Wonderful New Life.

Odette
x x x

THE CRYSTAL UNICORN

THE CRYSTAL UNICORN

Odette Volpelière-Pierrot

The Book Guild Ltd
Sussex, England

First published in Great Britain in 2004 by
The Book Guild Ltd
25 High Street
Lewes, East Sussex
BN7 2LU

Typesetting in Times by
IML Typographers, Birkenhead, Merseyside

Printed in Great Britain by
CPI Bath

A catalogue record for this book is
available from The British Library

ISBN 1 85776 873 6

ACKNOWLEDGEMENTS

G O D
Thank you

For the Love of my Family
My husband Dan
My children Joe and Lucy
and beyond

For all my friends
Past Present and Future

For all living creatures, that they may know freedom in their true state.

A special thank-you to Belle van der Linde for originally transcribing
my manuscript from longhand into type.

And for my friend Gloria Carter – A Healer and a Sensitive – for her
valued contribution to The Crystal Unicorn.
She suggested that I include the Creatures in the play, and we wrote
together Araya's speech on pages 53 and 54,
and it was she who composed the play's final two lines,
'The hands of time wrote this tale of fantasy and fame.
At heart we are all children creating.'

T H A N K   Y O U
A L L   M Y   L O V E

ODETTE

LIST AND DESCRIPTION OF CHARACTERS

NARRATOR
A very tall thin man; Merlinesque. His voice is without any particular accent, but he is well-spoken and kind.

THE MOTHER (in her thirties)

THE BOY ⎫
⎬ (twins approximately eight years old)
THE GIRL ⎭

THE CRYSTAL UNICORN
The Crystal Unicorn is carved out of crystal on the top of a mountain in the Gentle Land. It has the most beautiful voice, always in a slight echo. It is totally unjudgemental.

The Horses:

PALUSHA
A white female horse, with a beautiful mane and long thick tail. Her movements are fluid and gentle. Exudes an aura of calm (most of the time). There is a glow which always surrounds her. She is a Healer.

ZOR
A beautiful dark chestnut stallion with a glossy coat and thick mane and tail. His movements are more urgent and definite than Palusha's.

DRORK
A large horse, more thickly set than Zor. His colour is a dark, dirty maroon, and he has rounded shoulders and a very slight stoop. His movements are aggressive.

LINDEN
Palusha and Zor's twin son. Similar to Zor. Inclined to boastfulness but still has enormous compassion. A light glow surrounds him.

SARAI

Palusha and Zor's twin daughter. Similar to Palusha. She is possibly even gentler than her mother and has all of her attributes. A light glow surrounds her.

ZERO

Zor's friend and ally. A horse with a shiny black coat. He has an easy manner with Zor and is completely loyal.

ZIRROLA

Older 'working' horse, with a grey-brown coat. Absolutely no airs or graces.

The Droges:

DRERGEL

She is short and thick-set, has a round back, and is ugly in looks and manner. She is secretly in love with Drork but would never admit to it. She is a dirty dark-green colour. Her only outward concession to being a female is a large lumpy shoulder bag, which she also uses as a weapon.

DRERT

Similar in build and colour to Drergel but heavier. He is completely nasty. There is competition between them both. They are Drork's side-kicks and each wants to be his favourite.

All Droges have a wing like a bat's running along their spines.

OTHER DROGES

Nature Spirits:

YSOL

The Chief Nature Spirit, and the tallest. He is very kindly and has enormous patience and wisdom. Being an 'older' spirit, the colours of his clothes are softer than those of the 'younger' spirits. Less primary colouring.

CRELAH

Ysol's assistant. He specialises in astronomy. He has little patience with the young ones.

ZELAH
Female Nature Spirit. Older, she is a teacher, and always looks dishevelled.

LYDOOPY
A very young Nature Spirit. He is fairly naïve but progresses quite quickly. He is allowed to go around with the 'Elders' much to Crelah's annoyance.

LIRIPOOP
Young Nature Spirit, and leader of his gang. Jealous of Lydoopy and quite cruel towards him.

VARIOUS OTHER NATURE SPIRITS

The Creatures:

ARAYA MIDNIGHT SONG
A huge, very frightening spider. She is a bit hairy and the colour of rock, so, when necessary, she can crouch and look like a rock. She has the most beautiful gentle voice.

DANDY LONGLEGS
Male human – the only one. He is very tall, and quite affected. His clothes are flamboyant and colourful. He is totally disdainful of having to mix with the Creatures.

PERCE PENGUIN
A fairly lonesome chap. He hangs around the Mermaids trying to befriend and make conversation with them.

FROGS
Twin frogs called Left and Right. They croak their words. They spend all of their time marching. They also try out various arm movements.

BLUEBERRY PIE
American. She has a round blueberry body, and wears blue-and-white striped socks. She has a fabulous singing voice (and knows it), and is over-confident.

DESPERATUM HANKERFOLIUM
A tall willow-type tree. It is always crying and sobbing, and has hankies instead of leaves.

T'MERITY

A Bird of Paradise flower. A 'lady of the night', she has petals above her waist and wears orange satin tights. She is highly made up. She really does not care what others think of her.

CYRIL THE SQUIRREL

A grey squirrel with an outrageously large tail. A bumptious little 'geezer'.

BALD EAGLE

A small fat skinhead, with a feathery body. He wears a studded dog collar and has a Scottish accent. He is quite cruel and conceited.

FERDINAND FOX

A very smart and very English fox, who wears a red hunting jacket. Instinctively he knows he is a leader. He adores the Princess Perfecta.

ALI CAT

Tall skinny cat, with a red fez and a long nightshirt. He is not too sure of himself, and is in love with Vervain.

OLLIE OWL

Small round owl. He is an observer, saddened by all of the 'goings on' that he sees. He makes owl sounds using his wings.

THE PRINCESS PERFECTA

A shiny fat pig with a round tummy. She wears a tutu and a tiara, and carries a small sparkly wand. She does not sing, just dances. There is great rivalry between her and Blueberry Pie. Each believes that *she* should be the star. She is 'pig-headed'.

DOUG DOG

Bloodhound detective, who wears a dirty old raincoat. He does *nothing*; but the 'girls' adore him. He is quite sullen.

THE TWO MERMAIDS

Two long fair-haired Mermaids who sit in their shell. They are very floaty, with their arms moving in unison. Occasionally they get annoyed with each other if the other is out of sync, they cannot speak. They know that they are important.

FFEARLESS THE MOUSE

Small grey and very shy mouse, always hunched up and terrified. His only contact is with Desperatum, and is upset that the tree cannot stop crying.

VERVAIN
A very beautiful and *very* vain French striped tabby cat. She has fairly short but very thick fur. She wears a diamond-encrusted collar and red high heels. She cannot believe that she is not the centre of attention and that Doug Dog does not even acknowledge her.

VERVETTE
A replica of her mother but smaller. She follows Vervain obediently, accepting everything.

The Goddesses:

GODDESS OF THE EARTH
Long flowing dark-auburn hair. Her cloak and dress are in shimmering shades of bronze and green. She wear a golden wreath of woven leaves upon her head. Long fingers.

GODDESS OF THE SNOW
Long white/silver hair. Her flowing dress and cloak shimmer white and silver. She wears a tiara of sparkling icicles. Long fingers.

The scenery, clothing, make-up, etc. are of classical design, not modern or cartoonish.

I IN THE NURSERY

*A child's nursery. The style is traditional, but could be of any period –
Victorian, or Georgian, for example. There are two separate beds, one
child in each – the Boy and Girl. They are approximately eight years old.
At the front of the stage is a rocking horse, facing right.*

It is night-time, the children are sleeping. The Mother *gently opens the
door and enters. She is wearing nightclothes. She walks softly towards
the children – she kisses them, and as she turns away to leave, she spies
the rocking horse. She approaches and strokes it fondly.*

MOTHER   Oh darling wooden rocking horse,
how fast and sleek you stand.
Take me to the Lands with you,
your power in my hands.
Let's race through fields of dappled green,
and streams of sparkling blue,
and fly through clouds of darker shrouds,
beyond the deepest hue.
We'll fight a war against all wrong,
and gather up our forces,
and then we'll search and seek and find
all broken rocking horses.
Then when it's time to come back home
from journeys far and wide,
I'll lead you to where you belong,
right by my children's side.

Mists starts to swirl. Music plays, altering according to what the Narrator
says. Appropriate lighting, changing from dark to light etc.

NARRATOR   When daylight breaks and fairies wake,
and horses rise up from the lake,
when cobwebs shimmer in the sun,
and spiders know their food will come.
How much longer must they wait
before the spell of Drork will break?
Ten thousand waning moons ago
when raging winds brought driving snow,

and darkness fell, and death was born,
and black air hid the Unicorn,
in a cave far underground,
tied in chains, without a sound,
there stood a mare within this tomb,
two sparks of life within her womb.
Dazed and bruised from her abduction,
she now awaits the Drork's seduction.

[*All this takes place in mists, with only outlines and vague
shapes being visible.*]

It was forty hours ago
while bathing in her lake below,
that in her head, she saw the form
of the Crystal Unicorn.
A worried look within his eyes `
did tell that harm was in disguise.

CRYSTAL   To be alert and be aware
UNICORN   that danger comes in form of care.

[*When* Unicorn *speaks, pulsating light is visible.*]

NARRATOR   While walking through her open caves,
with light reflected from the waves,
she heard a sound she knew so well,
horse steps from the distant fell.
Cloaked in white across the mound
came guardians of the Greater Sound.
Swift and silent was their pace
as they approached Palusha's place.

CRYSTAL   To be alert and be aware
UNICORN   that danger comes in form of care.

NARRATOR   Too late to move and to react,
the Droges of Drork with wing of bat
did knock Palusha to the ground,
delighted with the prize they'd found.

DRERGEL   Our Drork will surely praise us more
now we have chained the *love* of Zor.

NARRATOR   Through the days and through the nights,
they forced their prize on endless flight.
Sights unseen and scenes unsighted
until, at last, the Droges alighted.

At this point the mists begin to clear and we can see the Tomb where
Palusha has been incarcerated. It is a large cave, decorated with cold
dark colours. There is a real feeling of chilliness. Palusha has been put in
chains, both ankles and wrists.

DRERT   The Doom of Drork, the Hill of Hate,
within this tomb you now must wait!

NARRATOR   Within a melting they had gone,
and left Palusha, alone and torn.

PALUSHA   What is this place so dank and cold?
What do they want that they must hold
me tied in chains like some poor thief,
with no more strength than a fallen leaf?

NARRATOR   The hours passed, and in her mind
she knew that Zor would come and find
and rescue her from this mistake.

PALUSHA   I'm not the horse they had to take.

II THE BANQUETING HALL
OF THE DRORK

The Banqueting Hall of the Drork. There are a few long tables. Like the Tomb, it has a dark and slimy feel. There are large tree roots, which give the effect of columns. Misshapen pieces of wood are used for seats, and on the tables are oddly shaped bottles. The Droges are drinking, arguing and pushing each other in a violent fashion.

There are two or three small 'bonfires', each some eighteen inches across, which are surrounded by several Droges, each taking a turn to inhale the fumes. As they inhale, they arch their bodies and stiffen. A few collapse after their turn. The Droge waiting to inhale is always impatient.

Torch flares are used for lighting.

There are a few Nature Spirits who 'melt' into the columns and walls, but are totally invisible until they move.

DRORK   Let's start the feast and eat the kill,
                  now victory's in our reach.
                  I'll slay that Zor ... but not before ...
                  there's a lesson I have to teach!

NARRATOR   That feast continued through the night;
                  the Droges got drunk on hate.
                  Some blood was spilt and stained the walls,
                  and Palusha awaits her fate.

DRERGEL   [*pointing to herself*]
                  I'm the one that's loyal to Drork;
                  I'm the one he needs.
                  You're just a jerk, an utter berk
                  filled with rotten seeds!

DRERT   [*hand on hip*]
                  Jealousy ... it really suits
                  [*admiring*]
                  a nice soft shade of green.
                  I'm the one who got the kill,
                  I'm the one who's been!

DRERGEL He's got *me* in his confidence;
things you would not believe.
He knows *I'd* give my life for him;
he knows *I'd* never leave.

DRERT Do you know who's guarding him?
Did he tell you *by the way*?
Do you think you're coming too?
[*pleased with himself*]
No! You're the one to stay!

DRORK [*raging with impatience*]
Stop! Stop it now, I say,
you should be as one!
Carry on like this some more
and *neither* is to come!

DRERGEL Oh Drork, dear Sir, Our Lord of All,
we really only jest.

[*The two are really fawning* ...]

DRERT You see we really are as one,
as Droges we are the best!

DRORK [*calmer and quieter*]
Fools, such fools, you fool yourselves;
not *me* you fool, your Master!
Just stop and stare and be aware
and learn a little faster ...

The day has come to light the fires
and sharpen up the knives,
and warn the world that Drork *is* God
and *make* them realise.
Go tell the guards that guard that wench
to leave her in no doubt,
that what I say is understood,
if she's *ever* to get out.

5

[Drork *waves them away.*]

NARRATOR   The Droges of Drork, with eyes of hawk,
set off underground,
to seek Palusha, tied in chains,
her freedom tightly bound.

III THE TOMB

The Tomb is very dark and cold. Palusha *is chained at her ankles and wrists. There is a small amount of straw for her bed. Other chains hang from the walls. There are stairs coming into the Tomb at the far end of the room.*

NARRATOR   Late that night, her silent screams
            resounded down below.

DRORK   I am the Drork, the Lord of All,
            and now you *really* know!

                                        [Drork *exits*.]

PALUSHA   [*lying down*]
            Where is Zor? Why does he wait
            to rescue me from here?
            I can't believe he'd ever leave
            me in this place of fear.

            [Palusha *is bruised, 'broken' and disorientated. Slowly she recovers enough to stand and sing.*]

PALUSHA   Take me down into the valley,
            take me where the waters flow,
            bring me a chaliceful of sunshine,
            bring me everything you know.

            Take my heart down to the valley,
            wash away my tortured fears,
            bathe my brow in virgin water,
            wash me in your salty tears.

            In the valley of the moonshine,
            lay my body down to rest;
            soothe my hurt and aching longings,
            touch me on my silver breast.

7

Think our minds away on moonbeams,
shadows lying down below,
weave away our minds from sorrow,
into the Silver Moon we know.

Pretend the world is an illusion,
that our reality's inside,
to have and hold in sweet seclusion,
a warm and gentle place to hide.

To face and look into each other,
with eyes that feel each other's pain;
to know there really is no other
love to share this love again.

NARRATOR   She is to wait a long long time.
Her sparks of life get born.
Two fine young foals, both bathed in light,
arrive one freezing dawn.

Quite a few moments of silence follow: Palusha *is giving birth. Her twins are born, both bathed in soft light.*

IV   THE OUTER REACHES OF THE GREATER SOUND

The Outer Reaches of the Greater Sound are quite bleak and barren: there are a few trees and some rocks. The sky is a light grey.

Zor and Zero are on reconnaissance of the Outer Reaches. All that they have with them are small rucksacks on their backs. Zor is pacing.

ZOR   There's something wrong, I feel it strongly,
     grey clouds within my mind.
     Palusha needs my help I feel,
     My God! I feel so blind.

ZERO   Zor, please don't go, you must be wrong –
     her area is manned:
     The Guardians of the Greater Sound
     do guard the Gentle Land.
     I gave instructions as we left
     to Zirrola and his son.
     They gave their oath, swords on heart,
     to guard Palusha's run.

ZOR   Then look for Ysol and his band,
     and ask him if they'll find
     Palusha, and the reason why
     that I should feel this blind.
     It's Drork ... I know his evil mind
     is coming through again;
     there's danger in the Gentle Land,
     danger ... and pain.

[Zero leaves.]

[Alone, Zor begins to sing:]

ZOR   Pitfalls and footfalls, demonic revenge,
     absurd vexations he sees in the sky.
     Lord of the Lantern, Destroyer of All,
     I am the one he intends to befall.

Bitter and twisted, unloved from his birth,
drawn to the darkness, like bats to the night,
feeding off evil ... vibrations of fear!
What is this feeling that's bringing him near?

[*beseechingly*]
Please give me the strength, whatever I need,
to do what I feel is about to become.
A voyage through darkness, which I feel is right.
Oh why can't I see the Unicorn's light?

Enter Ysol, Crelah, Lydoopy *and* Zero.

YSOL   The Gentle Land's in darkness;
the birds no longer sing.
The Drork has cast his shadow
across the Golden Ring.

They've stolen our Palusha.
The Droges, disguised in white,
bound and chained Palusha
and forced her on a flight.

Zirrola's badly injured;
he fought the Devil's fight,
to guard, protect his mistress,
from dark demonic might.

The Angels now have gathered
his son unto their wings.
The Droges did take his body
to feast upon and sing.

CRELAH   The Thirteen Pieces have been plundered
from the Crystal Cave.
The Unicorn is now in darkness;
the sentry's in a grave.

We saw the Droge attack the sentry,
and heard his evil laugh.
We saw him gloat at his destruction,
and admire the aftermath.

ZOR

[*thoughtful*]
Six pieces of silver and seven of gold,
the key to the Doom he has in his hold,
brought from a galaxy, eons away,
beyond furthest reaches from our Lunar Way.

[*becoming angry*]
And now Drork is laughing and planning attack
to stop me from getting Palusha back.
Somehow, with the help of the Unicorn's might,
we'll displace all the darkness and fill it with light.

YSOL

[*gently*]
Fear not for your love, for she is strong:
within her's the Love of the Lands.
The horses she's healed know of her plight
and the reason, she understands.
She chose to be the catalyst,
for this incarnation,
between the good, between the bad,
to dissolve the separation.

LYDOOPY

[*full of self-importance, thinking he may have something to add*]
Whatever the reason, whatever the season,
whatever's a girlish grin,
whatever's the pie that floats in the sky,
whatever the mood we're in.

[*He begins to sing:*]

I'm feeling *so* evolved, I'm feeling *so* evolved
that I have solved
the problem of the Lands.
I'm feeling *so* evolved, I'm feeling so *ev*—

CRELAH

SHUT UP!

ZOR

[*ignoring this interruption*]
We must leave this place and journey on,

11

back to the Greater Sound,
and then on to the Gentle Land
across that fateful mound.
Arrange a force so skilled and fine
that nothing can destroy,
and when we're as one with many eyes,
[*with quiet determination*]
then we shall deploy.

NARRATOR　　Preparations were made for the Journey of Dark.
In thousands they flocked to the Lands.
The selections were tough, the majority failed;
her fate was to be in their hands.
Many months passed by; Zor's force was trained
in ways of defence and attack,
in visualisation of the imagination,
and dissolving the Forces of Black.

Ancient horses of war from the Lesser Sound
came to divulge information.
With Zor now their leader, their New Crusader,
they honour their obligation.
Ysol and his band scoured the Lands
for kin with talents unique –
of tele-transference and stellar observance,
and the power to strengthen the weak.

V   THE TOMB IN THE DOOM OF DRORK

The Tomb has altered slightly. There is nesting material, and it is not so gloomy.

Palusha is sad. She thinks that her twins, Linden *and* Sarai, *are asleep, but they hear her song.*

The twins are beginning to grow up. They are adolescent.

PALUSHI   Until I looked into his eyes,
             I did not realise,
             what pain that love could bring.
             To never touch or hold his face,
             or ever be embraced again.
             Does he not know that he has twins?
             Two fine young foals from his own limbs ...
             and from our love.

They come across to gently change her mood.

LINDEN   Tell us of the Unicorn.
             Tell us of his might.
             Tell us of the Golden Days,
             when the Lands were bathed in light.

SARAI   And then we want to hear of Zor,
             of miracles untold,
             how you and father fell in love,
             and of the Ring of Gold.

LINDEN   And hear of Ysol and his band,
             and how they can commune
             with Nature and the Elements,
             and of the Silver Moon.

             [Palusha *settles down to tell her story.*]

PALUSHA   The Unicorn lives way up there,
             [*she points*]
             his head up in the sky,

carved from crystal pure as snow,
where ancient horses fly.
He's there for all; he doesn't judge
the rights or wrongs we do,
and when we ask him for his help,
his voice comes shining through.

Just close your eyes and visualise
a face so warm and strong,
and feel inside, enormous pride,
knowing we belong.

And Zor, your father, how we met
one summer's day in spring.
He came, leaning on some friends,
his leg *in* the Golden Ring.

He'd been invited by the Clan
from the Lesser Sound,
to receive the Golden Ring,
which made him Honour-Bound.

While travelling back, the group of friends
began to horse around.
They forced the Ring onto his leg
while pinned upon the ground!

A minor tragedy ensued
whilst on the journey home:
he caught the Ring upon a branch,
whilst falling off a stone!

[*more slowly*]
When he arrived at where I live ... lived! –
my home is here with you –

[Palusha *gets up and stands slightly away from the twins.*]

and when I saw his face, those eyes,
came a feeling I felt I knew ...

[*dreamily*]
On a throne of rock he sat,
eyes piercing mine;
an early memory
divine.
An Earth God
clothed in nothing
ornate,
a simple skin,
he sealed my fate.

He stayed and stayed for many weeks
saying his leg still hurt,
not wanting me to be with others,
... and how he did flirt!

[*She returns to her children.*]

Enough's enough, for now awhile
it's time you had a rest.
Remember all that I have taught
for when you have your test.

Sarai *is at the back of the stage looking towards an entrance that we cannot see. Gradually* Araya *comes into view. She is a* very *large spider.*

SARAI   [*she screams*]
              Arrrgh!

Sarai *and* Linden *rush to* Palusha.

ARAYA   Don't be afraid of me, please don't!
              I know I do look scary;
              I've spent all morning making sure
              that I don't look *too* hairy.

LINDEN   Mmmu!

PALUSHA   Sshhh ...

15

ARAYA   [*moving slowly towards them*]
             My name's Araya, 'Midnight Song',
             and I truly do believe
             that if you let me help your plight,
             then I can help you leave.

PALUSHA   Who ... how did you get here?
             When did you arrive?
             How come the Droges of Drork
             let you through alive?

ARAYA   I am of no consequence to them;
             they leave me well alone.
             When they start their violence
             I turn into a stone.

             [*She demonstrates her ability to change into stone.*]

             I slip unnoticed through passageways,
             go down into the deep
             and enter into chambers where
             the Nature Spirits sleep.

             They're unaware, the Droges I mean,
             that Nature Spirits are
             inhabiting these lower spheres,
             blessed by an Avatar.

             They *too* become invisible
             when up amongst the Droges.
             They're *very* unpredictable
             those sly bedevilled rogues.

PALUSHA   [*approaching* Araya]
             Zor ... have you had news of him?
             Is he still alive?
             Does he know I'm in the Doom
             and that I did survive?

16

[Palusha *approaches* Araya, *but the twins stay put, looking extremely worried and uncertain.*]

Does he know that he has twins,
foals both bright and strong?
Can you get a message through?
Oh please try, Midnight Song!

ARAYA

Please don't despair, Palusha!
Zor knows that you are here.
He's really doing all he can
to take you from this fear.

He's training hard a force quite mixed
of different evolutions,
and getting through that finite truth,
the Reality of Illusion.

He's yet to know about his twins;
he doesn't know they're born,
There's only One who'll tell him so –
the Crystal Unicorn.

PALUSHA

[*moving away and with a sad-sounding voice*]
This place was not always dark and evil.
I sense a glow that once shone bright,
an incandescence, a luminescence,
that filled these caves and passageways with light.

ARAYA

Years ago, beyond the mists,
a young prince was born.
He was never held, and never kissed;
he spent those years alone, forlorn.

[Araya *is beginning to settle in.*]

When early manhood then arrived,
his heart was in distress.
Nothing then could touch his soul,
save for the Dark Princess.

17

He knew that this, at last, was love
that nothing could destroy;
he'd found a mother, wife and child,
he'd found his final joy.

The more he gave, the more she took,
the stronger she became,
till finally she walked away
and left him half insane.

He vowed from then he'd never give,
he'd only ever take;
that there was nothing he couldn't have,
and no one he couldn't break.

He decided too, to change his name,
to become more like a hawk;
to live and breathe within the dark,
. . . to become the Drork.
[*She gives a resigned shrug.*]

VI IN THE GREAT HALL

The Great Hall is in the Greater Sound. It is rather like an old-fashioned village hall, but there are no seats.

Dandy Longlegs – the only human – is ushering all the Creatures *into the hall. They are to stand in a straight line.*

DANDY L'LEGS This way please and hurry up!
No, *no*, in a line!
I really shouldn't be doing this,
mixing with dogs and swine.

Well now! As you are well aware,
you all *failed* the selections,
but ... the consensus is,
you may form a special section.

Pay attention, please!
Three birds and a dog,
a squirrel, two frogs,
two mermaids, three cats and a flower,
two rodents, one fruit, a pig and a pile of damp wood.

DESPERATUM [*clearly upset*]
No, no!

DANDY L'LEGS Oh very well then ... Tree!

[Princess Perfecta *pirouettes from the line.*]

[*pointing to* Princess Perfecta]
Swerve back, you swine!

PRINCESS P. [*looking puzzled*]
Swerve?

DANDY L'LEGS [*sarcastically*]
Swerve: to depart from
a straight line.

19

FERDINAND *Names!* We have *names*. Don't you *know*
that we have names? You anthropoid!
[*aside*]
Clearly from the wrong evolution.

DANDY L'LEGS I demand RESPECT; I shall *have* respect;
I *deserve* respect.

DOUG DOG Sure!

BLUE. PIE [*singing*]
I think we should sing a song,
to welcome her when she returns
back to the Lands where she belongs ...

[*small applause*]

Oh! And *I'm* Blueberry Pie.
[*curtsies*]

DANDY L'LEGS You'll give *me* your names,
and no games! From left to right.

FROGS [*croaking*]
Left.   Right.

[*The* Frogs *march out of the line while giving their names.*]

DESPERATUM [*weeping uncontrollably*]
Desperatum Hankerfolium.

T'MERITY [*hand on hip*]
T'merity.

SQUIRREL Cyril.

BALD EAGLE Bald Eagle.

FERDINAND
FOX Ferdinand.

20

ALI CAT   Ali.

OLLIE OWL   Ollie.

PRINCESS P.   [*enunciating clearly with a toss of her head*]
The Prin-cess Per-fect-a.

DOUG DOG   Doug.

Mermaids *just sway their arms and bodies. Their hair is very long and floats. They move in unison and do not speak. They sit in a large shell.*

DANDY L'LEGS   [*pointing to* Mermaids]
Your names?

[Mermaids *continue to look floaty but say nothing.*]

DANDY L'LEGS   [*disdainfully*]
Are you at home? . . . Huh!

FFEARLESS   [*terrified*]
F-f-f-fearless.

DANDY L'LEGS   Oh yeah!

VERVAIN   [*both hands on hips, one hip out; pursed lips*]
I'm VERVAIN.

DANDY L'LEGS   That's true.

VERVETTE   Vervette.
[*She performs the same action as her mother.*]

PERCE   Perce.
PENGUIN

DANDY L'LEGS   What? Short for Perce the Peng!
Form groups quietly and quickly
and decide what you're going to do!
You're lucky, you know, to be given this chance;
there were *thousands* who didn't get through!

21

[Creatures *choose with whom they want to be.*]

[T'merity *is chatting up* Doug.]

T'MERITY   [*to* Doug Dog]
How interesting! I work undercover at night too!

[Vervain *walks past dragging* Vervette.]

VERVAIN   [*to* Doug Dog, *holding her nose*]
Dug something up?

[*There is real competition between* Blueberry Pie *and* Princess Perfecta.]

BLUE. PIE   [*to* Princess P.]
So what are *you* gonna do? *Miss Perfect*?

PRINCESS P.   With these cloven hooves of fire, I shall inspire
Palusha to dance, and entrance her with my grace
as no other in this place can do ... and you?

BLUE. PIE   Just sing ... simply sing and bring
a new dimension of sound around the ground
where I perform ... that's all!

FFEARLESS   [*to* Desperatum]
It's all-all-all right.

DESPERATUM   But it's not all right ... it never *is* all right.

FFEARLESS   Why do you cry?

DESPARATUM   It's what I do. Its my purpose in life.
I'm here to absorb sadness, despair and
grieve for the pain that others can't see.
I'm alone in my sorrow ... so alone. Leave me be.

[Ffearless *does not know whether to go or stay.*]

PERCE   [*to* Mermaids]

22

Good afternoon, ladies. I don't actually blame
you for not telling him your names.
[*He pauses.*]
Do you have difficulty conversing ...
[*He pauses.*]

[*The* Mermaids *ignore him and continue swaying.*]

PERCE   ... underwater? Mmm?

[Ferdinand *is feeling* Cyril's *tail as if it were cloth.*]

FERDINAND   [*to* Cyril]
A fine brush you have there, good-quality hair.
Allow me to introduce myself. Ferdinand Fox.
Master of Underburrow. Greater Sound. At your ser*vice.*

[Cyril *is bumptious; a real little 'geezer'.*]

CYRIL   Cyril the Squirrel of Whatever-You-Fancy. Ha!
So, er, what's your state of play in the order of things
appertaining to this here assembl*age*?

FERDINAND   Directing, producing and keeping the points of crisis to a
minimum.

BALD EAGLE   [*to* Ollie]
What do you reckon on that mouse then?

[*He regards the mouse as a good meal.*]

OLLIE   D'knowww.

[Ollie *is not at all interested.*]

BALD EAGLE   Scrawny legs, don't suppose he can run too
fast ... no fun in that!

ALI   Yeah.

[Ali *is only half paying attention; he is transfixed by*
Vervain.]

23

BALD EAGLE   *[nodding, very pleased with himself]*
This isn't really my flight of fancy you know, not my thing at all, this isn't, but I dare say Zor needs all the support he can get, and us, being here, doing all this, must be very reassuring for him.

VII   THE DOOM OF DRORK

Drork's *quarters are better than* Palusha's. *There are furnishings, though their colour is heavy and dark. Whilst he is singing the song, he is preening himself in front of a 'cheval mirror'. This mirror has the head of a horse carved at the top.*

DRORK
The measure of pleasure I get from destruction
surpasses the climax derived from seduction.
The ultimate *joy* to destroy all that's sacred
can only enhance my esteem.

I'm baiting and waiting for Zor to enter
my centre of darkness and torture and laughter,
to retrieve all the Pieces I took from the Unicorn,
Oh yes! [*laughs*] And rescue the *Nag*. [*sneers*]

Sometime in the Tomb should mellow the fellow,
unloosen his *good* in which he can wallow
and swallow his pride that his bride
is no longer his . . . hmmmMarvellous!

Enter Drert *and* Drergel, *clapping.*

DRORK
[*furiously*]
How *dare* you spy and sneak in here!
How *dare* you creep about!
If you have words you want to say
then come . . . *spit* them out!

DRERGEL
[Drergel *is nervous but quite excited.*]
The Pieces, Sir, you know the ones.

DRORK
[*sarcastically*]
No – tell me about them!

DRERGEL
Well, do you remember when . . .

DRORK
Arrrgh!

25

DRERT   [*fawning*]
Oh Lord of All, let *me* explain
why we kept out of sight:
the Pieces from the Crystal Cave
are becoming *awfully* bright.

DRERGEL   There's something strange and sinister
that's happening in that cave –
I became quite beautiful,
benevolent and brave.

DRERT   [*grimacing at* Drergel]
It made me ill to see the smile
that spread across her face.
She said I looked ethereal,
and that I moved with grace.

The awful thing ... I must admit ...
I felt a warmth inside,
a feeling so extraordinary
that I almost cried.

DRORK   [*exasperated*]
Save me! Help me! Give me strength!
Before I kill them both ...
These Droges of Drork are close to death
and *that* you have on oath!

Go down and bring that wench up here, and
[*very threateningly*]
never let me find
you creeping round and listening to
the secrets of my mind. NOW!

Oh! And *do* be careful when you pass
the Pieces in the cave;
I'd hate to think the power therein
could *ever* make you brave!
[*laughs*]

[*Exit the* Droges.]

Drork *now adopts a meditative position and speaks quietly.*

DRORK

Come Zor, concentrate!
Within this point of space,
I have your heart's desire with me.
Look ... envisage her face!

[*becoming angry*]
I'll not be ruled by female ploys,
nor take their words as oath,
nor relinquish how I may feel,
nor ever plight my troth.

[*with disgust*]
Such deceit, lies, hidden there
behind those declarations.
With impunity they feign
total adoration.

[*He hears a noise; then, a few moments of silence.*]

[*half crazy*]
Again! It's happened again!
These creeping lurking peasants.
Can no one knock, or even cough,
to alert me to their presence.

Enter Palusha, *singing calmly and gently.*

PALUSHA

Take off your mask and show me your truth;
break down your walls and believe you'll be safe.
Hiding from nowhere where nowhere exists,
crouching in mist where denial persists.

I'm not here to harm you, nor weaken your power
nor make you a promise I know I can't keep.
Such anger and hurt, I know, comes from pain.
I'll not offer contortions nor pledges profane.

27

Take what is painful and hold it right here.
[*she points to her heart*]
Change it from darkness to lightness and warmth;
surround it with light and feelings of love.
You need only ask to get help from above.

[*even gentler*]
Engage not more conflict nor actions of rage.
The behaviour of those who deem it all right,
can only behave from examples they've known,
and often have spent many years all alone.

DRORK   [*sarcastically*]
Oh! so you think you know something, do you?
Something you haven't been told!
Is it *me* you refer to or perhaps someone else?
Dear! Your comments are becoming quite bold!

PALUSHA   I know what I feel, and what I feel, I believe in,
and what I believe in is right.
It's not only physical senses that function,
there's also the unseeing sight.

DRORK   So! Tell me my future! What do you see?
My heart filled with love or with hate?
Do you think I'll become Lord of the Lands?
Tell me this fantasy–fate!

PALUSHA   You create your own world, by the thoughts that you have;
your actions are born in your head.
Why must you keep me down in the dungeon?
What do I have that you dread?
Trapped here with you, I'm freer than you,
your shackles don't do what you hope,
we're not born to ignore the gifts that we have,
nor strangle the life force with rope.

DRORK   [*quieter, his eyes narrowing with curiosity.*]
Why don't you hate me? Why don't you scream?
Why don't you lose control?
How come this confinement deep underground
hasn't demolished your soul?

28

PALUSHA   He comes to me at night.
In dreams I dream he loves me.
In dark the truth is spoken
the words I long to hear.

[Palusha *sings this while looking at* Drork.]

He hold our heads together,
a sad look in his eyes;
a love to live in darkness
a love daylight defies.

[*She looks away.*]

Don't come to me in sunshine
nor look at me through rain.
The moon can be our guardian,
while we can love again.

Maybe it's a rehearsal,
for a lifetime to be,
to recognise each other,
to love when we are free.

[*She turns away.*]

Don't leave my dreams to wander.
Don't lock away the moon.
Be there in hours of darkness,
back in our Silver Moon.

VIII   INTO THE PARASELENE

The Paraselene is a dome-shaped room with two jade thrones. The only other objects are golden glowing orbs of light. Everything else is glowing white. Palusha, Sarai *and* Linden *off-stage. Only their voices can be heard.*

SARAI
How come you named us what you did,
and knew we'd be one of each?

LINDEN
… And was it very difficult
to teach us the power of speech?

PALUSHA
One night whilst I was fast asleep,
I travelled to the stars,
and on my journey into space
I saw a moon near Mars.

[*There is a feeling of travelling through space; then a bright glow in the distance.*]

A bright spot shone, a Paraselene,
a warm and gentle light,
that instantly I changed my course
and glad I did that night.

Palusha *enters through a doorway; the two* Goddesses *become visible.*

When I arrived upon that moon
a doorway opened wide;
two voices called and beckoned me
through to the other side.

SARAI
[*still off-stage*]
Who was there?

LINDEN
[*off-stage*]
What did you see?

30

PALUSHA   I stepped across into a hall
           filled with golden orbs of light,
           and sitting there on Thrones of Jade
           were images so bright.

           [*The Paraselene is very, very bright, and when* Palusha
           *enters she has to shield her eyes. Then a shadow falls, but
           the Paraselene does not become gloomy.*]

           And then as if a shadow fell
           to enable me to see,
           two Goddesses on Thrones of Jade
           called and beckoned me.

           [Palusha *walks towards the* Goddesses.]

           The Goddess of the Earth, she smiled
           and said:

GODDESS OF   You'll have a son,
THE EARTH and when you leave the Doom of Drork
           his work will have begun.

           He'll harness Nature in his hands
           and heal destruction done.
           No matter what he has to face,
           there's nothing he will shun.

           He'll leave a mark where he has been,
           invisible to most,
           but there's something he may *never* do,
           and that is *never* boast.

           One day, in the future when
           it's time he leaves your side,
           then you can know within your heart
           that I shall be his guide.

           [Palusha *turns to the* Goddess of the Snow.]

31

PALUSHA And then the Goddess of the Snow
wept a gentle tear,
and told me, though the Drork was dark,
that I should have no fear.

She said:

GODDESS OF I see a girl inside
THE SNOW whose affinity's with snow,
who understands the Master Plan
of where the waters go.

I'll teach her how the rain is formed,
and its effects in space,
and no matter where it has been
it will always leave a trace.

And show designs we need for snow
that fall upon the seas,
and how to alter such designs
for snow that falls on trees.

A different snow protects the buds
that bloom in early spring,
from the snow that starts to fall
when peacocks cease to sing.

[*The* Goddesses *vanish into glowing mists.*]

PALUSHA And then quite suddenly,
and yet it seemed quite slow,
The Goddesses of Snow and Earth
dissolved into a glow.

I called out to where they were,
to thank them for what was told,
but they had gone, and what was left
were just the orbs of gold.

32

LINDEN   [*off-stage*]
Were you frightened?

SARAI   [*off-stage*]
Did you cry?

PALUSHA   A little, and no.
So, I left the Hall of Golden Orbs
and passed back through the door,
but in my mind I felt, perhaps,
that there was something more.

[*There is the feeling of travelling through space again.*]

And as I left that magic moon
and travelled into space,
I heard their voices once again,
but from a different place.

The Goddess of the Earth she said:

[*The voices of the two* Goddesses *come from different places in the theatre.*]

GODDESS OF   Linden is his name.
THE EARTH   I shall protect and guide your son
but he *must* respect his name.

PALUSHA   Then the Goddess of the Snow
called out your name:

GODDESS OF   Sarai,
THE SNOW

PALUSHA   and said:

GODDESS OF   When she needs to contact me,
THE SNOW   just call up to the sky.

Their learning will be done at night
when they are fast asleep
so when their time has come to work,
their awareness will be deep.

[*The bright glow ... and the Paraselene vanish.*]

PALUSHA   I turned around to say goodbye,
          but there was nothing there.
          The Paraselene where I had been,
          had vanished into air!

IX   IN THE CRYSTAL CAVE

The Crystal Cave is situated deep inside the mountain, above which is carved the head of the Crystal Unicorn. *It is a fairly small cave and very light. The entrance at the back of the stage glows with deep blues. In the centre, hewn out of crystal, is an altar. On the altar is a crystal bowl, which, though now empty, once contained the Thirteen Pieces.*

NARRATOR

Deep below the Unicorn, far down underground,
in the still of the Crystal Cave, where Zor is often found.
Fighting thoughts inside his head, enemies within,
deciphering corrupt ideas, from the genuine.

[Zor *is pacing the floor and is fairly agitated.*]

ZOR

God, how I feel her pain, how I feel my own!
After what she did for me, I left her all alone!
I had no need to make that journey,
although she said I should –
sometimes surveying the Outer Reaches,
she said, would do me good! Huh!

CRYSTAL
UNICORN

Take a light and shine it bright,
and search for reflections within.
Do not despair! Araya's there
to help her and her kin.

ZOR

[*calmer*]
Had she not been taken,
had I had a wider view,
maybe I'd have sired a foal,
maybe even two!

Oh what's the use in wondering
the ifs, the buts, the whys?
I must continue imagining,
piercing those darker skies.

[*with a sudden burst of anger*]
How I detest that morbid mind
that filters into space,

[*softer*]
Oh Unicorn, please hear my voice;
please let me see your face.

[*He thinks he can hear* Palusha's *voice, as if echoing from a great distance:*]

PALUSHA'S
VOICE

Don't come with hate,
I'd rather wait.
[*quieter*]
Don't come with hate,
I'd rather wait.

[Zor *leans against the central altar, looking preoccupied.*]

CRYSTAL
UNICORN

Light balls of energy flash through the sky,
preparing the path ahead.
When you dissolve all this anger inside you,
you'll harness new strengths instead.

Hold tight the light and spirit free;
from dawn to dusk, we are
your eyes and ears and senses three
to journey you afar.

ZOR

[*with growing spirit*]
Zor *can* and *shall* fly through the night
with power in his wings,
and trust the voices in his head,
and hear the voice that sings.

I *shan't* bestow a morbid thought,
nor enter into deeds,
that weaken hearts and multiply
those dark pernicious seeds.

My army flies out into space
with Zero at my side.
There's not a crack or crevice where
the Drork shall ever hide.

[*with vigour*]
Oh thank you, Unicorn, for being there,
for sharing of your love.
I promise now, for what I'm worth,
to restore your Light above.

Zero *knocks and enters.*

ZERO   May I enter? Do you mind?
I was feeling bored outside ...
There are stories going round
I think should be denied.

They say the army's more than ready,
impatient now to fight;
that you are now procrastinating,
and likely taken fright.

ZOR   [*shocked*]
They've what?! They've said I've taken fright? ...
[*laughing*]
My belly's turned to fear?
[*pondering*]
Yes ... I think it's time
[*decisively*]
to tell the journey's near.

I'll not be long; don't wait for me!
I've one more thing to do.
To redefine what's in my mind,
to make it strong and true.

[Zero *leaves*]

Zor *is walking around clearing his head. He begins to sing, his voice full of emotion and feeling.*

ZOR   My love, can you hear me?
Can you feel my heart?
Listen ... in the silence,
I shall soon depart.

37

Hold on, please don't give up,
don't despair of me.
I long to touch you,
hold you and be free.

Love like we have
is born of many lives.
Know that it's real,
and soon I shall arrive.

Remember our Silver Moon;
we'll go there again.
Holding you, holding me,
released from pain.

In my head, I see us with
two fine young foals ...
Is this a hope, a fantasy,
a reflection in my Soul?

The longer that we are apart,
I cry for you.
No greater love there can exist ...
I'd die for you.

X IN THE CLEARING

The Clearing is in the Greater Sound. It is a large open space in the middle of a wood. There are chair-shaped rocks and moss-covered stools. Honeysuckle and ivy drape the trees.

Ysol is waiting for Crelah *in one of the chairs.* Lydoopy *is already with him.* Crelah *arrives.*

YSOL
Ah Crelah! There you are!
What's your information?
Do the Planets bode us well
by your divination?

CRELAH
Yes, I think I know the time,
and it's coming soon,
when we will all have congregated
on the Boundary of the Doom

The cycle of the sun and moons
at the moment that they cross.
when all is plunged in total darkness,
the moment of Saros.

LYDOOPY
[*full of self-importance*]
And if we *miss* this important moment
and *if* you've got it wrong,
when do we have another Saros?
I *assume* it won't be long!

CRELAH
[*snappily*]
Eighteen years eleven days and eight hours!

YSOL
[*gently*]
I can't imagine he's got it wrong;
his mind is far too clear.
He's more at home up in the Heavens,
up in the Outer Sphere.

[*to* Crelah]
Have you spoken yet to Zelah?
How has she progressed?
Has she put them through their paces,
and did they pass her test?

CRELAH   It's not been easy; their concentration
was in a pretty awful state.
She's had to take them back to basics
which has made her lifeline late.

She feels now that they should be ready
for your approbation,
so when you know you have some free time,
she'll hold the examination.

YSOL   Let's make it now, let's not delay.
If you could find her soon,
to have the neophytes pass their test
would be most opportune.

[Crelah *leaves to look for* Zelah *and the neophytes.*]

So Lydoopy, while we wait,
what have you got to tell?
Did you use the full moon's lighting
and did you weave that spell?

LYDOOPY   I really tried my very best
and nearly got it right,
but just as I was incantating
the moon shot out of sight!

YSOL   [*a look of gentle surprise*]
Oh yes?

LYDOOPY   [*not* quite *whining, and looking sorry for himself*]
Well, I was really concentrating
and calling out aloud,

and just about to weave my spell,
when the moon hid behind a cloud.

I was really disappointed,
dejected and depressed,
thinking, 'What's the use of even trying?'
[*brighter*]
when I saw Celeste.

She said that I was not to worry,
that she would help repel
the disappointments and dejections,
that demoralised my spell.

YSOL   [*kindly*]
I'm sure with help now from Celeste,
and *knowing* where you went wrong,
you'll weave your spell quite beautifully,
and keep your persistence strong.

As spiders go, Celeste has flair
for weaving spells sublime.
[Ysol *is not admonishing* Lydoopy.]
You *really are* a lucky chap
that she's giving you her time.

Enter Crelah.

CRELAH   I found them just beyond the clearing;
they're on their way right now.
The neophytes are quite excited,
but poor Zelah's anyhow.

Enter Zelah, *looking completely dishevelled,* Liripoop *and other* Nature
Spirits. Ysol *beckons to* Zelah.

YSOL   Zelah, can I have a word?

NATURE SPIRIT   [*nudging* Liripoop and pointing to Lydoopy]
Hey Liripoop!

41

LIRIPOOP   [*to* Lydoopy]
Oh look, there's the professor!
What a *fine* young man he be!
His intelligence is quite astounding,
our Professor of Morology.

[Liripoop *pretends to butter up* Lydoopy *and feigns to be in awe of him.*]

Come, Lydoopy, let us share
the secrets in your head.
We'd *so* love to be your friend,
not your adversary instead.

LYDOOPY   [*frowning and uncertain*]
What is it you want to know?
How to weave a spell?
[*with more confidence*]
Or shall I teach you of the Saros
[*very confident*]
and where the fairies dwell?

LIRIPOOP   [*very pleading*]
Anything, just anything,
everything you know.
Any wisdom from your lips
can only help us grow.

[Zelah *overhears the last two lines:*]

ZELAH   [*furiously*]
Liripoop! Come here!

[Lydoopy *walks slowly over to* Ysol *looking questioning and sad.*]

LYDOOPY   [*to* Ysol]
Excuse me, please, what does Morology mean?

42

YSOL   [*gently*]
Stupid talk ... why?

[Lydoopy *shakes his head and walks away.*]

XI   IN THE TOMB

Palusha *and the twins are sitting in the formation of a triangle. She is giving them a word test.* Palusha *has her back to the audience.*

PALUSHA East wind?

LINDEN Zephyr.

SARAI That's the west wind.

PALUSHA You and me equals us; that's the clue.

LINDEN Eurus!

PALUSHA Creophagist?

SARAI and Urr! Flesh-eater!
LINDEN
together

PALUSHA A bright spot or mock moon,
    seen in connection with a lunar halo?

SARAI A paraselene ... is where I've been,
   and seen the Queens of Jade.

PALUSHA Yes, very good!
    Fohat?

LINDEN Cosmic electricity, primordial light, the
    universal propelling vital force.

PALUSHA Good.

LINDEN [*very pleased with himself*]
    It's brilliant!

PALUSHA   [*admonishing*]
               No boasting!
               The bottom part of a graduate's hood?

LINDEN   Liripoop!

PALUSHA   Equinox?
               [*she pronounces it* equine-ox]

SARAI   The twice-yearly celestial occurrences,
               when the physical, emotional, mental
               and spiritual aspects of all horses reach
               their highest points of attainment.

PALUSHA   Well done!
               A malt beer brewed by the ancients?

LINDEN   [*laughingly*]
               It's *zythum* that gives 'em rhythm!

PALUSHA   Saros?

SARAI   A cycle of eighteen years, eleven days
               and eight hours, after which period the
               relative positions of sun, moon and
               moon's node recur, so that the
               eclipses can be precisely predicted.

PALUSHA   Soap? ... No? Well, it's possibly
               an old mare's tale,
               but on Earth where humans live,
               it's a substance that they give
               to children who, when too bold,
               are told to wash their mouths out with.
               Apparently it cleans the words.
               And lastly the name Grayson?

LINDEN   It's the name used by men on Earth
               who started a liaison,
               whose ancestors lived in the Greater Sound
               who altered their name to Grayson.

45

PALUSHA   You have done extremely well
           and both deserve a treat.
           I want you now to close your eyes,
           and surrender into sleep.

           [*The twins curl up and* Palusha *strokes them until they fall asleep.*]

XII   DREAMSCAPE

Sarai *and* Linden *are standing side by side in the centre of the stage, facing slightly outwards. They are shielding their eyes in the clearing mists. At first, there is no colour, only white. Gradually small wisps of colour float by. They try to catch them. They succeed and hold the wisps up in wonderment. (This is the first time they have seen 'clear' colour.) They then carefully place each wisp of colour into two small piles on the floor.*

Sarai *begins to wander and sees something float past her. She touches it and it bursts. It is a floating puddle. She jumps back exclaiming and laughing. (All in silence; there is only music.) She looks at* Linden's *back. He turns, and she bursts another floating puddle. He finds one and tries it, poking it with his finger; it bursts. He finds another and claps it between his hands, laughing.*

Gradually a rainbow has been forming in the background. Linden *notices it and turns to* Sarai. *She looks. Suddenly they hear loud cracks. Pieces of the rainbow break off and shoot through the air. It is a rainbow storm. More and more floating puddles appear and more wisps also, until the atmosphere is 'full'.* Sarai *and* Linden *are catching pieces of rainbow firecrackers, bursting puddles and trailing the wisps. All this is performed like a 'loose' or informal dance.*

The Goddess of the Earth *and a linden tree appear out of the mist at the side of the stage, and* Linden *approaches it slowly.* Sarai *does not notice this. The voice of the* Goddess of the Earth *speaks to* Linden *but only he can hear.*

GODDESS OF   Look well and learn.
THE EARTH   Listen and feel.
             Absorb and understand.
             Know the structure.
             Use the correct voice vibration
             and store the scent.

Linden *stands for a few moments longer, then turns and looks at* Sarai. *She looks at him. He turns to show her the tree, but there is nothing there. He sits down somewhat puzzled, his head in his hands.*

On the opposite side of the stage to where the linden tree was appears the Goddess of the Snow *and a waterfall. The sounds of water are as of tumbling crystals.*

47

There then appears silver rain around Sarai. *She opens her arms and throws her head back, loving the sensation. Slowly snow begins to replace the rain, each flake being a different crystalline shape. She stands there under the falling snow.*

GODDESS OF   Touch and feel.
THE SNOW   Watch the melting.
                Listen to the changing.
                Observe the traces in the air.
                Notice the scent of each shape
                and remember.

Sarai *closes her eyes for a few moments and, on opening them, looks at* Linden. *He turns ... there is nothing left but the white mists slowly enveloping everything. The music fades. Just as* Sarai *and* Linden *are about to disappear into the mists, the image of the* Crystal Unicorn *appears.*

CRYSTAL   This is what dreams are made of,
UNICORN   so plan your dreams with care.

XIII   THE TOMB

The twins and Palusha *are in exactly the same position they were at the end of the previous Tomb scene.* Araya *enters. She is excited.*

ARAYA   Palusha, can we talk?
There's something you ought to know.
Are you sure the twins are fast asleep ...
I know when you're to go!

PALUSHA   Leave here! To go home?

ARAYA   Yes, the Nature Spirits far below
are in communication
with their kin back in the Lands
regarding your liberation.

PALUSHA   When? Do you know?

ARAYA   The moment of Saros is when
they'll form their congregation,
on the boundary of the Doom
to observe his 'exhumation'.

When 'He' and Zor are in combat,
Saros shall then take place,
and you, my dear, with the twins
will have to run your race.

You'll have the Thirteen Pieces then,
and they shall give you light,
and you must somehow get to Zor
to make his darkness bright.

That is all that I can tell,
but do feel deep inside,
that you and your beloved twins,
do have a Leading Guide.

49

I must be off – there's work to do
and things to finalise –
and make quite sure what is prepared
won't be compromised.

XIV ON THE BOUNDARY OF THE DOOM

*The Boundary of the Doom is very bleak and gloomy. There are some
dead trees. Occasionally something flies past emitting dreadful sounds.*
Zor *glows with light.*

ZOR

What a cold and dismal place!
How does anything survive?
What creatures choose to live in this?
There's nothing here alive!

Zero, have you seen Zirrola?
I really wasn't sure
if he was fit and strong enough
to pay his final score.

ZERO

He's all right, he's bearing up;
I saw him over there.
The only thing disturbing him
is breathing in this air.

[*He beckons to* Zirrola, *who comes immediately.*]

ZOR

Ah Zirrola, here you are!
You're feeling strong enough?
Judging by this atmosphere,
things should get fairly rough.

ZIRROLA

[*with quiet determination*]
I'm well enough and strong enough,
with resolve to avenge my son.
Until I've got *him* in my hands,
my work down here's not done.

ZERO

Will you recognise him
in this dreary grey?
Heavens knows what we shall see,
and what we shall survey.

ZIRROLA I'll know that face, those eyes, that stench,
that disgusting sound he made.
He's burnt a hole right in my soul;
now's *his* chance to be afraid.

[Zor *puts his arm on* Zirrola's *shoulder in an
understanding gesture.* Zirrola *then walks back to his
original place.*]

ZERO Do you suppose Palusha knows
how close we are to her?
Maybe she already knows
through a messenger.

[Ysol *starts to cross towards* Zor.]

ZOR I dare not hope or even think
of what lies ahead.
The emotions in my stomach are
like storms inside my head.

YSOL It's almost time that Drork was here;
we've heard he's on his way.
Good luck, Zor, I bid you well,
and wish you everyway.

XV   THE TOMB

Palusha *is standing with arms outstretched. Her mood is almost happy and is much lighter.*

PALUSHA
Paradise: a world above the clouds,
reached through darker shrouds
Where Beings sing and send a light glow through
into the world down here, of deeper hue.
Calling, falling, in open space,
charging atmosphere with electric grace.
Being, seeing, omnipotent sight,
freefalling, glorious flight.
Away on the winds, cobwebs blown,
deep in a mind a seed is sown.
Waking, taking a feathered friend
with plumage like the rainbow's end.
Hairy, scary feelings fly,
through my head and through my eye.

[Linden *and* Sarai *are much more subdued.*]

LINDEN
Through dark infected zones where lost souls converge,
let daylight infiltrate and purge.

SARAI
How long will it be before we are free,
taking the darkness down?
The ships sail by, the horses cry,
and even the mermaids drown.

Enter Araya *holding the Pieces. She has threaded them into three necklaces using her cobweb. The necklace with five pieces is given to* Palusha *and those with four pieces to the twins.*

ARAYA
Pearls of wisdom I hang before your face,
priceless jewels, unseen, untouched by human hands.
Do you see them all of you? Then here, take a strand.
[*she gives out the necklaces*]
Held by gold and silver threads they are
made from angels' wings, hung upon a star.

53

Threaded, beaded works of art,
shining, glowing, from end to start.
Take a strand, pull it taut;
savour each and every thought.
May the end then stand in sight.
May the darkness shine through light.
To know, whatever gloom is there,
The Unicorn is ever fair.
May the mistress of the dawn
light you with her golden hair.
Sorrows trenched and sorrows deep,
maidens underground can weep.
Take it, break it, do as you will;
now is your chance to have your fill.
Place them now upon your breast
and hide them not from sight.

[Palusha *and the twins hang the necklaces around their
necks.*]

Let them come and let them see
their all sustaining light.
Make it, shake it, dance with three,
take your chance and follow me.

The twins *immediately start to follow* Araya.
   Palusha *instinctively turns around to check she has forgotten nothing
and also gives a slow last look.*

XVI   THE BOUNDARY OF THE DOOM

There are distant rumblings. Zor's *army has now gathered into fighting groups, with the* Nature Spirits *strategically placed. All are standing alert, as the final few fighters get into position. The music becomes 'darker' and louder. After a couple of tense minutes,* Ysol *begins to speak. The fighters slightly incline their heads as they listen.*

YSOL   Concentrate, focalise your mind.
        Take slow deep breaths.
        Harness your strength to this point.
        [*points to the heart*]
        There *is* only success!
        Prepare ... Now!

The Droges *rush in screaming and shouting and making gurgling noises, attacking and rushing at everything.*
    Slowly creeping out of the foray come Drergel *and* Drert *not looking at all sure. Suddenly,* Zirrola *sees* Drert. *He rushes over to him, trying hard not to shake and lose control.*

ZIRROLA   [*grabbing* Drert *by the shoulders*]
          It's *you*, it's *you*, isn't it!?
          You killed my son!
          Have you no conception
          of what you have done?

          You've torn my life
          limb from limb
          destroyed my son
          just on a whim!

          [*pushing* Drert *away, and in a more controlled voice*]
          Well! Now we meet!
          What have you to say?
          Do you have a magic word
          to make it go away?

55

DRERT   [*half cringing and half trying to look bold*]
I ... er ... *he* attacked *me*.
It was self-defence!
I'll do anything you ask
in way of recompense!

ZIRROLA   Recompense! Recompense!
You not only *killed* my son,
you *ate* him too!
Maybe that's the answer ...
[*he approaches* Drert *in a very threatening manner.*]
I'll do the same to you.

Drergel *rushes up and start to whack* Zirrola *with her shoulder bag.*
Zirrola *constrains her.*

DRERGEL   No ... no you can't ...
He's not well ...
It's those Pieces;
he's under a spell.

ZIRROLA   [*taking a step backwards and looking stunned; much
quieter*]
Is this what I've waited so long for?
This combat to the death!
The avengence of my son.
You're not worth my breath!

Drork *enters and calls out to* Zor.

DRORK   Zor ... [*laughs*] Welcome to my kingdom!
Welcome to the Doom.
Plan on staying long?
Or maybe leaving soon.
[*shakes head*]

Palusha's *very* comfy,
has *no* desire to leave,
I have a surprise, or two, in store,
and what ... you could not conceive.

[Drork *is baiting* Zor.]

There's no need for combat!
[*beckoning to* Zor]
Just follow me ... this way.
I'll show you to your chamber where
you *shall* enjoy your stay.

ZOR   You think it's all so easy;
a command is all you need.
You think I'd leave Palusha
to satisfy your greed.

I've come to take Palusha
from this awful gloom,
and *no one* is to stop us now
from fleeing from this Doom.

CRELAH   Now!

Saros takes place. The boundary is plunged into total darkness. The Droges laugh and cheer. Zor's *army is being beaten; their eyes are not accustomed to the darkness.* Ysol's *voice rings out.*

YSOL   Don't try to fight them;
just try to restrain them!

The fighting continues. Liripoop *is in trouble. The darkness has become less dense.* Lydoopy *goes to his defence. The light is gradually becoming brighter.* Lydoopy *deals with* Liripoop's *adversary using 'laser' vision. He then walks away and continues to battle. The light suddenly becomes very bright as* Palusha, *the twins and* Araya *appear. The* Droges *are blinded, stumble and shield their eyes.* Linden *passes his row of the* Pieces *to* Araya ... *he runs into the foray.*

Zor *is now in real combat with* Drork. Linden *gets close and stops a* Droge *from felling* Zor *from behind.*

The Droges *are doing their best to fight whilst shielding their eyes from the light.* Zor *turns to* Linden *and nods a thank-you. The following conversation takes place whilst they are overpowering* Droges.

LINDEN   Hello, Father!

ZOR   Hello ... Who are you?

LINDEN   Your son!

ZOR   Sorry?

LINDEN   Your son!

ZOR   [*laughs*]
            Oh yes? ... How come we haven't met?

LINDEN   We've been living with Palusha.

ZOR   You know Palusha?

LINDEN   Yes ... She's my mother.

ZOR   Your what?

            [*On hearing this news,* Zor *has renewed strength and
            momentarily disables* Drork.]

LINDEN   My mother ... and Sarai is my sister ...
            your daughter.

ZOR   My sister ... your daughter!

LINDEN   No. *My* sister *your* daughter!

ZOR   You mean ...?

LINDEN   That's right!

ZOR   [*grabbing* Linden *by the shoulders in amazement*]
            My son? My son!

            [*All the while* Zor's *army have been tying up the* Droges
            with ropes. Drork *slopes off.*]

ZOR   Where's Palusha? Is she here?

LINDEN   Over there with the others.

Zor *stumbles over and around fighting* Droges *and slowly approaches* Palusha. Palusha *gently pushes* Sarai *towards her father.*

SARAI   Hello ... I'm Sarai.

ZOR   Hello ... I ... I'm ...

He hugs her and then, whilst hugging her, looks at Palusha. *He approaches* Palusha *and they hug and hold each other not saying anything. They pull apart.*

ZOR   Thank God you're safe.

PALUSHA   Oh Zor! Mr darling Zor ... How I've longed ...

             [Zor *begins to sing. All the while,* Zor *is holding* Palusha *and looking at her.*]

ZOR   My heart awaits you in our golden dreams.
Beyond the realms of Earth we lived our love.
through starlit skies with eyes that smiled with tears,
we travelled through the blue on wings of dove.

The angelic chorus sing of what they know.
Is it Heaven that has sent you to my door?
That makes me wait for fate to take a hand?
To strengthen what in me was weak before?

Dare I look at you in these daylight hours?
Can I resist, desist, your loving eyes?
Is it wrong to long to touch my heart's desire?
And do I lose the chance to claim my prize?

                           [Araya *disappears.*]

If all can call and ask the Gods for help
and know the truth of what we feel inside,

then I await my fate with burning joy
for days to come that have been prophesied.

[Linden *bounds across*.]

LINDEN   So you've all met?

PALUSHA   Oh yes! Er ... No!
            Araya ... Where's Araya?
            Araya ... Araya?

ZOR   Who's Araya?

Re-enter Araya.

PALUSHA   Araya ... Come and meet Zor ... come!

            [Zor *takes a step backwards.*]

PALUSHA   Zor, this is Araya ... Araya Midnight Song.

            [Zor *is slightly stunned ... then he approaches* Araya.]

PALUSHA   Araya ... Zor!

ARAYA   [*shyly*]
            Hello, Zor.

ZOR   Hello!

            [*He goes to take her hand but does not know which one
            to take.*]

PALUSHA   It is Araya who saved our sanity.
            She brought us gifts of Love.
            She made the darkness lighter,
            and brought us news of you, from above.

She came when my faith was straining,
and gave news of your journey's plans.
My dearest Araya Midnight Song,
with *many* helping hands.

[Araya *is looking extremely embarrassed.*]

ZOR [*to* Araya]
I believe I owe you an enormous debt.
What in the Unicorn's name can I do?
Just tell me your wish and I'll do all I can
to make your desires come true.

ARAYA [*very awkward*]
Oh nothing, please nothing, there's nothing at all;
the honour is totally mine.
How many spiders are given this chance
to share in this moment of time?

By now most of the Droges *have been tied up and have been or are being
pulled into heaps.* Liripoop *approaches* Lydoopy.

LIRIPOOP Er ... Lydoopy ... er ... What you did back there ...
... Thanks a lot.
I'm really glad you noticed
that I was in a spot.

LYDOOPY It's nothing.

LIRIPOOP There's something else ... I'm sorry
for the sarcasm I displayed.
I really do feel badly
and hope you'll forget the charade.

LYDOOPY Amnesia has now taken place!

[Lydoopy *and* Liripoop *acknowledge each other as friends
by holding shoulders and inclining heads.*]

In the meantime Araya *has returned the Pieces to* Linden, *who is wearing
them around his neck.*

61

ZOR   I think it's time to start to plan
the journey back, quite soon.
I'll tell them all to take their rest
for departure this afternoon.

[Zor *crosses to where* Ysol *is.*]

PALUSHA   Araya, please come with us,
back to the Gentle Land,
to share our life, and share our home,
and leave this dismal land.

ARAYA   This spider's song won't last long;
I've one last task to do.
I can't leave now, but know we'll meet
before our time is through.

NARRATOR   Through the days and through the nights
they winged their way on triumphant flight,
seeing sights and sighting scenes,
exchanging tales of what had been.

How things had changed back in the Lands,
the work of Ysol and his band;
how all therein were made aware
of Palusha's plight and her despair.

How darkness fell and death was born,
when black air hid the Unicorn;
with Pieces gone from the Crystal Cave,
and Palusha chained to be a slave.

And how Araya saved the day,
whisking the Pieces clean away,
from the Cave far underground,
to be returned without a sound.

XVII   IN THE CLEARING: THE CELEBRATION

The Clearing in the Gentle Land has been transformed into a baroque setting: columns are draped with garlands; the ground is strewn with flowers, and tables are laden with fruits, cakes, etc. In the distance the head of the Crystal Unicorn *is glowing, vibrant on the mountain top. The* Creatures *are getting ready to welcome back* Palusha, Zor *and their children.* Dandy Longlegs *is leaving the stage.*

FERDINAND   [*to* Cyril]
Posturing there in garments so fine!
Referring to Princess Perfecta as swine!

[Princess Perfecta *stomps daintily over and gives*
Ferdinand *a pathetic little smile.*]

FERDINAND   Such grace ... that face!
I wonder if she'd consider an embrace?

[*She pauses and half offers her lips, then immediately swishes her hair and walks away wiggling her bottom.*]

FERDINAND   [*wagging his finger*]
She's a very naughty girl!

CYRIL   She's got real style ...
and a lovely smile.

PERCE   [*to* Mermaids]
So ... as you don't sing,
what will your contribution be?

[*The* Mermaids *wave their arms, exasperated.*]

PERCE   That's it?

[*They clasp their faces and look at each other.*]

63

FFEARLESS [*to* Desperatum]
Will you cry in time to the music?

DESPERATUM I don't know ... I really don't know ...
It's all too much!

T.MERITY [*to* Doug]
If you come over to my place,
I'll show you where I keep my pollen.

[Doug *chokes on his cigarette*, Vervain *having witnessed this*]

VERVAIN [*to* Vervette]
Some *dogs* be'ave like *men*!
Come, *chérie*!

[Ali, *having watched all this, approaches* Vervain *and reads from a scrappy piece of paper:*]

ALI Excuse me, M'dame ... I've er ...
I know that I'm not 'ansome.
I know that I'm not sleek.
I know you fancy Doug Dog.
I know I've got a cheek.
But down along my alley,
where I lay my 'ead to rest,
I wondered if you're willing,
to come and be impressed?

[Vervain *throw her hand to her forehead, half collapses and stumbles away.*]

BALD E. [*to* Ollie]
What d'you call a dark horse?

OLLIE Don't know.

BALD E. A nightmare!
[*laughs*]
I've heard Palusha's had a few!
[*nudging him*]

OLLIE   A few what?

BALD E.   Nightmares!

OLLIE   [*turning to face* Bald Eagle]
          Do you have many friends?

BALD E.   [*bewildered*]
          Huh?

          [Ollie *walks away sadly.*]

Enter Blueberry Pie, *followed by* Dandy Longlegs.

BLUE. PIE   They seek me from afar to sing.
          I aim to be the star and bring
          accolades and rapturous applause,
          from here to far-off shores.

          [Princess P. *hears this and looks furious.*]

PRINCESS P. They seek *me* from even *further* away to dance.
          There's no one here to take away *my* chance,
          to shine and make the evening *mine*!

          [Dandy Longlegs *is listening.*]

DANDY L'LEGS Any more trouble from you two,
          and I'll ban *you* from wearing your tutu,
          and *you* can be quiet before there's a riot
          [*he looks at his watch*]
          Right, that's it, they're due.

All the Creatures *hurry to their positions. Gradually all of the* Nature Spirits *arrive, together with the horses who went to the Doom. When they have all arranged themselves,* Zor, Palusha *and the twins enter, the twins looking incredulously at the surroundings.*

    There is a great rejoicing in the Clearing. When the applause is over, Zor *begins to speak.*

ZOR   The darkness brings a host of things
that horses' eyes can't see.
I thank you Ysol and your band
for being there with me.

To Zero and Zirrola,
such bravery renowned,
whatever I can do for you
I am Honour Bound.

To the Crystal Unicorn
I have this to say:
thank you for guiding me
and bringing me this day.

And to Araya Midnight Song
I owe my greatest debt,
for recovering the Pieces
whilst under dire threat.

[*with arms outstretched to all the* Creatures]
I thank *you, too*, for being here,
and this wonderful display,
and I don't think any one of us
shall ever forget today.
Thank you!

Great applause from everyone, then the music starts. Ferdinand *takes up position as conductor.* Blueberry Pie *and* Princess Perfecta *are at opposite ends of the line, checking each other out. The* Creatures *begin to perform their song.* Princess Perfecta *pirouettes and gives little leaps and makes a 'big deal' of dancing in front of* Blueberry Pie. *The* Mermaids *have now acquired floaty scarves to wave.* Ollie *makes owl noises with his hands.* Desperatum Hankerfolium *wails and cries in time to the music. The* Frogs *march in time.*

ALL   Welcome! Welcome home, back to the Gentle Land.
CREATURES   How we have missed you, Palusha,
and your healing light.

We would have liked to make the journey
and all joined in the fight,
but we all failed the selections;
we guess we weren't quite right.

BLUE. PIE We guess we weren't quite right!

ALL But now you're here and so are we,
CREATURES your new life can begin,
and as we're here and so are you,
a welcome to your twins!

BLUE. PIE A welcome to your twins!

ALL We tried another kind of song,
CREATURES while you were stuck in jail,
and realised you wouldn't want
an operatic gale.

BLUE. PIE An operatic gale.

[*She takes a huge curtsy.*]

[*Applause from everyone.* Palusha *steps forward.*]

PALUSHA I thank you from my deepest heart
for this celebration.
How I dreamed of being home,
While in that incarceration.

[*very gently*]
He could have killed me, Linden and Sarai
whilst living underground,
and realise the changes here
[*she places her hand on her heart*]
are really quite profound.

We must *forgive* when we are wronged
and *not* desire revenge,
not physically, not mentally;
just leave it unavenged.

67

I realise the choice *was* mine
before this incarnation,
maybe to redress a wrong,
to earn a vindication;

That every thought and every deed
and every word we speak
are our responsibility
and make us *strong* or *weak*.

And Zelah, dear, you had a job,
a *great deal* to achieve.
The neophytes who did so well
excelled in make-believe.

Thank you, Zor, for being you,
and coming to the Doom,
not knowing you had sparks of life
born into the gloom.

ZOR   How could I not come
when you are all I want,
breathing every breath,
for you?

Nothing now can part
one being made as two,
two hearts in tune together
for ever.

PALUSHA   I am here for now,
for now and ever more.
Let nothing in this life
destroy us.

Know that we are safe,
no longer in the dark;
that no grey clouds
can ever cast their shadow.

PALUSHA and ZOR together   Through pain has come a love,
a love we can rejoice in,
a love that shares each moment
completely.

[*They beckon to* Linden *and* Sarai.]

Come, Linden and Sarai;
let's share this ride of life.
We will do our best to guide you.
We cannot stop the pain
that has to touch your hearts,
but you can know our love's
beside you.

ZOR   [*to* Linden]
The Goddess of the Earth
will take you by your hand,
and let you understand,
and teach you.

PALUSHA   [*to* Sarai]
The Goddess of the Snow
shall teach you what to know:
how crystals correlate
to water.

ZOR and PALUSHA together   But more than all of this,
we have a bright new dawn;
a chance, right here, to recreate.
Believe in who you are
in all that you can do,
and always listen to the voice
within you.

Applause from all – then murmurings as all look towards the entrance.
Araya enters followed by Drork, Drergel *and* Drert. *A stunned silence*
follows. Araya *approaches* Palusha, Zor *and the twins.*

ARAYA   I did say we'd meet again.
         I wouldn't break my word:
         that I had one last task to do
         before I am transferred

         [*Small gasps and murmurings from the crowd. The look
         of hate and evil is leaving* Drork. *His features seem to
         change; his body is altering.*]

DRORK   [*softly and disbelieving*]
         What is the transformation
         that amazes all around?
         As if snake-like a skin starts to fall . . .
         An amazing transfiguration,
         beyond my wildest dreams.
         [*quietly*]
         I feel reborn! I live again!
         As if let out of jail . . .

         Sensations new, vibrations, too,
         I feel within this form.
         A light, I feel, grows in my heart,
         and outwards to the world.

         [*He then takes a small step forward, and the crowd
         recoils.*]

         I've seen what hate,
         I've known what hate,
         I've felt what hate can do!
         Don't shut me out;
         I've come this far . . .
         I need help from you.

         [Lydoopy *now fetches* Liripoop *and goes to stand near*
         Drork.]

LYDOOPY [*to* Drork]
         The world alight has gone to flight,
         the heavens open upwards.

70

The bird has flown, the wind has gone,
and Mankind waits to save us.
The Breast of the Earth, the Soul of Loving,
the hands of God unite.
We turn around and to the ground
we pour our love and light.
A Saviour waits to show the way;
the path is grazed and broken.
We struggle on, all hate has gone,
and Heaven will have spoken.
We cancel Life, we cancel Death
and try to block our feelings;
but deep inside, no place to hide,
a touching on our feelings.
A bright light comes; the Devil's gone;
a passage clear and wide,
to love and laugh, to kiss the hearth
from where the fire is healing.
[*to the crowd, indicating* Drork]
Go get the man and show him all,
and stand him straight and true;
[*to* Drork]
and slowly when the darkness can
his chains begin to fall.
And take this man and hold his hand
and visions to his eyes;
the world can go, his Soul can grow
and Heaven realise.

Palusha *and* Zor *walk slowly towards* Drork. Palusha *then offers her forehead to* Drork *in the sign of welcome.* Zor *then does the same. As* Zor and Drork *part,* Zelah *calls out.*

ZELAH   Look ... Araya!

[Araya *is weakening; she is speaking with difficulty.*]

ARAYA   The deepest wounds within the heart
are healed by passing time ...

71

and then ... as if by magic ...
[*she is panting*]
... my midnight hour is here.

[Araya *dies. A stunned silence followed by soft weeping and murmuring.*]

NARRATOR ... and so Araya passed, in time untold,
into the fold
of heavenly awareness.

XVIII   IN THE NURSERY

It is now morning. The Mother *enters . . . opens the curtains and her twins wake up. She looks towards the rocking horse, which has moved and is now facing left. She looks puzzled.*

MOTHER   Did you sleep well, darlings?
                   Did you have any dreams?

BOY   Yes!

GIRL   [*looking at her brother*]
                   I think it was a dream.

As the curtains close the Crystal Unicorn *says:*

The hands of time wrote this tale of fantasy and fame.
At heart, we are all children creating.